NOAH'S BARK

For my family —S.K.

Pour Filou —R.

Carolrhoda Books
A division of Lerner Publishing Group, Inc.
241 First Avenue North
Minneapolis, MN 55401 U.S.A.

Website address: www.lernerbooks.com

Library of Congress Cataloging-in-Publication Data

Krensky, Stephen.
  Noah's bark / by Stephen Krensky ; illustrated by Rogé.
      p.   cm.
    Summary: Noah is distracted by animals making whatever sound comes into their heads while he is trying to build, then pilot, the ark, and so he devises a way for each animal to choose only one sound.
    ISBN: 978-0-8225-7645-7 (lib. bdg. : alk. paper)
    1. Noah (Biblical figure)—Juvenile fiction. [1. Noah (Biblical figure)—Fiction. 2. Noah's ark—Fiction. 3. Animal sounds—Fiction. 4. Deluge—Fiction. 5. Humorous stories.] I. Rogé, 1972– ill.
II. Title.
PZ7.K883Noa 2010
[E]—dc22   2007010022

Manufactured in the United States of America
1 – JR – 12/15/09

NOAH'S BARK

Stephen Krensky

illustrations by Rogé

Carolrhoda Books · Minneapolis · New York

baah baah

Long, long ago,

when people were still few and far between,
the world was full of confusing sounds.

Mostly, the animals made it that way.
They were loud and silly
and said whatever came into their heads.

hissssssssss

roooooarr

Beavers crowed when the sun came up.

Snakes quacked in distress.

QUACK

quack
quack!

Pigs howled at the full moon.

And mighty elephants hissed in fear.

All this noise was a problem for Noah.
He was trying to build an ark,
and it was hard to concentrate.
"I NEED QUIET!" he barked.

"There's work to be done."

meeeow meow

hee-haaw

neeeeeeeiiiiiigh

hooonk

cock-a-doodle-dooooo

Then it started to rain.
And rain and rain and rain.

Some of the animals
grew frightened.

hissssssssssss

rooooarr

hoot hoot hoot

Luckily, Noah had finished his work.
He told the animals about the
great flood that was coming.

"But don't worry," he said, "you will
all be safe on my ark."

Some of the animals believed him.
Others did not.

The ones that did got in line
and climbed on board.

The rain continued to fall.

Pretty soon, the puddles were ponds, the ponds were lakes, and nobody could tell where the lakes ended and the oceans began.

And then the ark was afloat.

The rain went on and on.
But now a great wind rose up as well.
It tossed the ark about
in the angry seas.

Down below, the animals were crowded together, trying to keep their pointy parts to themselves.

Still, the rain didn't stop.

Thunder roared and lightning flashed
as strong winds tossed the ark about.

Noah was worried.

Would the ark hold together?

Or would it sink to the bottom of the world?

Noah asked the animals
to help—and they all
answered at once.

neeeeeiiiiigh neeeiiiighhh

HiiilSSSSSSSSSSSSS

meow meow meeeoooow

hoooooooooo

baah baah baaah baaah

ooooo mooooo

SSSSSSS ooowl

his

chirp chirp

quack qua

"QUIET!" Noah barked.

And for once, the animals grew silent. "We'll never survive this way. Something has to be done."

And then Noah had an idea.

He borrowed a turkey feather to write a list
of all the animal sounds he had ever heard.

Then he asked the toucan to cut the list into pieces.

Finally, he put the pieces into the kangaroo's pouch.

"Each of you will pick out one
sound," he explained.
"From now on, that
will be the ONLY
sound you'll
make."

Each animal took a turn.

"Hooooowwwwlllll?" cried the wolves.

"M-mooooowww," the cows stuttered.

"Bah-bah-pah-pah," said the sheep, shaking their heads.

Now Noah quickly gave directions.

The pigs oinked if anyone fell overboard.

The parrots squawked when a big wave was coming.

And the lions roared when the roof leaked.

Rooooarr

Squuuaaaawkk!

Noah was pleased.

He could tell who was
who and what was what.

The weeks to come were still dangerous,
but now the animals were able to work together.

After forty days and forty nights,
the sun returned to the sky.
The waters fell, and the ark came to rest.
It was time for the animals to leave.
Two by two, they thanked Noah for saving them
and for giving them their own special sounds.

12/10
E KRE